To Paula
C. F.

Lofty
Brachiosaurus

Scratch
Tyrannosaurus rex

Sniff
Monoclonius

This edition published by Parragon Books Ltd in 2014 and distributed by

Parragon Inc.
440 Park Avenue South, 13th Floor
New York, NY 10016
www.parragon.com

Text and Illustrations © Charles Fuge 2013

ISBN 978-1-4723-4605-6

Printed in China

Three Little Dinosaurs
Egg Rescue!

Charles Fuge

PaRRagon

Bath · New York · Cologne · Melbourne · Delhi
Hong Kong · Shenzhen · Singapore · Amsterdam

"Look!" said Scratch to his friends Lofty and Sniff.
"I'm going to have a new baby brother or sister!"
Mrs. Rex stood up. There was a beautiful
egg in her sandy nest.

"Will you look after the egg
while I take a shower?" asked Mrs. Rex.
"Don't let any naughty mammals near it!"

Off she went. But it wasn't long before a snuffling,
whiskery snout poked out from the undergrowth.

"Mammal!" squealed Sniff.

"Playtime!" cried the mammal and snatched the egg.
"Quick!" shouted Scratch. "After him!"

The three little dinosaurs raced
after the naughty mammal ...

"Gotcha!" cried Scratch.
But the egg shot straight out
of the mammal's arms ...

sailed through the air ...

and landed **PLOP!** in the river.

The three little dinosaurs stared in horror.

"What do we do now?" cried Sniff.

Scratch hurried to the river's edge.
"Look! We can use that tree trunk as a raft!"

"Go!" shouted Scratch.
They paddled with all their might.

But the current was getting stronger,
and they could hear a thunderous roar ...

"WATERFALL!" yelped Lofty.
Scratch reached out and grabbed the egg.
He held on tight.

Then
the
three
little
dinosaurs
began
to
fall.

Down
and
down
they
fell,
until …

BUMP!

... they suddenly stopped.
They had landed right on
top of Mrs. Rex's head!

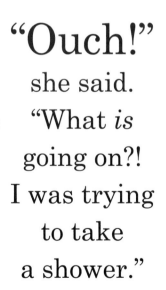

"Ouch!"
she said.
"What *is*
going on?!
I was trying
to take
a shower."

The three friends
told their story.

Scratch held up the egg.
It was cracked!
But Mrs. Rex just smiled.
"Look!" she said.
"It's not broken ...

"... it's HATCHING!"

A baby dinosaur was chipping its way out of the egg.
It looked straight at Scratch, blinked, and smiled.

"Mama!" it squeaked.

The three little dinosaurs collapsed in a heap of giggles.
"I'm not your mama!" laughed Scratch.
"I'm your big brother,
and I'm ready to play!"